DISNEY's

A Winnie the Pooh First Reader

Pooh's Book of Adventures

Stories by Isabel Gaines

DISNEP PRESS

NEW YORK

Contents

DISNEY'S

A Winnie the Pooh First Reader

Pooh's Honey Tree

Adapted by Isabel Gaines

ILLUSTRATED BY Nancy Stevenson

—

Pooh's Honey Tree

Winnie the Pooh

was a bear of little brain.

But he had a big,

loving heart.

And a big,

round tummy.

Pooh's tummy always looked

quite full.

But it always felt

quite hungry.

Hungry for honey!

One day Pooh went

to the cupboard

and got out his honeypot.

There was nothing left

but the sticky part.

Suddenly, Pooh heard

a buzzing sound.

BUZZ! BUZZ! BUZZ!

"That buzzing means something,"

said Pooh.

Something small and fuzzy

flew past his ear.

BUZZ! BUZZ! BUZZ!

"Oh!" said Pooh. "A bee!"

Now, it is true

that Pooh was not very smart.

But one thing he knew:

where there are bees,

there is honey!

So . . .

Pooh followed the bee

deep into the Hundred-Acre

Wood.

Soon they came

to a tall, tall tree.

A honey tree!

Up the tree Pooh went.

Up.

Up.

Up.

Then, CRACK!

A branch broke.

Down the tree Pooh fell.

Down.

Down.

Down.

Pooh rubbed his sore head.

All that head-rubbing

made Pooh think.

And the first thing he thought of

was Christopher Robin.

Pooh picked himself up

and set off to find

his friend.

When Pooh got

to Christopher Robin's house

he looked

at Christopher Robin's bike.

A big blue balloon was tied

to it.

"May I borrow your balloon?"

Pooh asked Christopher Robin.

"I need it to get some honey."

Christopher Robin gave Pooh

the balloon.

"Here, Pooh.

But you can't get honey

with a balloon," he said.

"Oh, yes, I can," said Pooh.

"I will hang on to the string

and float up to the honey."

"Silly old bear," said

Christopher Robin.

"The bees will see you.

They will not let you near

their honey."

"Yes, they will," Pooh said.

Pooh and Christopher Robin

went back

to Pooh's honey tree.

Next, Pooh sat down

in the mud and rolled around.

Soon he was covered

with mud from his nose

to his toes.

"Look!" Pooh said.

"The bees will think

I'm a little black rain cloud.

They will not even know

I am there."

"Oh," said Christopher Robin.

He sat down

under the honey tree

to see what would

happen next.

Pooh held on tight

to the big blue balloon.

Then he floated

all the way up

to the top of the tree.

Pooh tried to act

like a little black rain cloud.

He hung by the tree

for a long, long time.

Then he reached

into the hole

and pulled out a pawful

of golden honey.

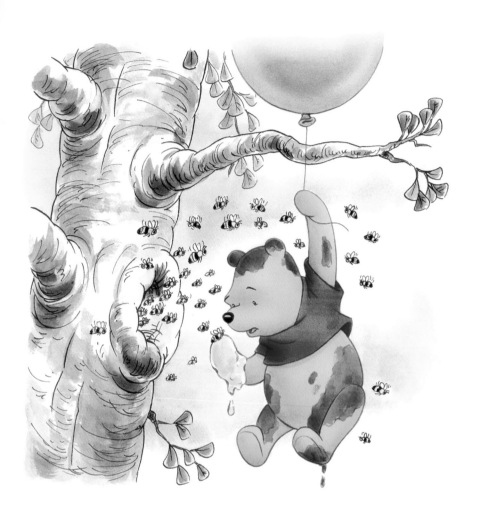

BUZZ! BUZZ! BUZZ!

The bees began to buzz

around Pooh's head.

They were not fooled at all.

29

All of a sudden,

the balloon string

came undone.

Pooh hopped onto the balloon

before it could get away.

Then Pooh and his balloon

sailed over the treetops.

Then the balloon

lost all its air.

Down it came.

And down came Pooh.

This time, Pooh landed

right on top

of Christopher Robin.

Pooh looked up at the bees

in the tree.

Then he looked down

at Christopher Robin.

"Oh dear!" Pooh said.

"I guess it all comes

from liking honey so much!"

A Winnie the Pooh First Reader

Pooh's Leaf Pile

by Isabel Gaines

ILLUSTRATED BY Francesc Rigol

Pooh's Leaf Pile

One lovely fall day,

the air was cool and crisp.

So Pooh and Piglet decided

to play outside.

They stepped out Pooh's door.

As they walked,

Pooh heard a strange

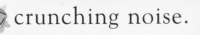 crunching noise.

"Piglet," said Pooh,

"do you hear that noise?"

Pooh and Piglet stopped and listened.

But they didn't hear anything.

"Look!" said Pooh.

"The trees have lost

all their leaves."

They continued on their walk.

Crunch crunch, they heard again.

"Piglet," said Pooh,

"I believe that noise

is the sound of our feet

stepping on the leaves.

See, they've fallen to the ground."

"Oh my!" said Piglet.

"Look at all the colors."

Just then, Rabbit arrived.

"Pooh!" he cried.

"Look at your yard!"

"Isn't it pretty?" said Pooh.

"Your yard is a mess," said Rabbit.

"We must clean it up.

Get the rakes!

We will rake the leaves

into one big pile."

"But they look so pretty," said Pooh.

"They will look pretty in a pile, too,"
said Rabbit.

Pooh, Piglet, and Rabbit
raked and raked and raked.

As they finished,

Tigger and Roo stopped by.

"That's a terrific leaf pile,"

said Tigger. "Perfect for bouncing!"

Tigger and Roo bounced

into the pile of leaves.

Pooh and Piglet jumped

into the pile, too.

"Roo," said Tigger,

"let's tell everyone

about Pooh's leaf pile."

Tigger and Roo bounced off

to get the others.

"Oh no!" Rabbit cried.
"Our neat pile of leaves
is now a big mess!"
"Perhaps we should
do something else
with them," said Piglet.

"Yes," said Rabbit.

"Something that's not so messy.
Let's ask Christopher Robin
what to do."

Everyone gathered around Pooh's leaf pile.

They waited for Rabbit

and Christopher Robin.

When they finally arrived,

Christopher Robin said,

"Let's make crafts with the leaves.

First, we will make a collage."

All the friends gathered

leaves, acorns, pinecones, and nuts.

Christopher Robin helped them

paste everything onto

a big piece of paper.

"Great job!" said Christopher Robin.

Next Christopher Robin
had everyone tape leaves
onto a piece of paper.
Then they painted the paper,
leaves and all.

When they were done painting,

they carefully removed the leaves

from the paper.

"Leaf shapes!" said Piglet.

For the last craft,

everyone placed a leaf

underneath a piece of paper.

Then they peeled the paper wrapping

off a crayon.

They rolled the crayon

over the paper.

"A leaf appeared on my paper!"

said Roo. "It's magic!"

"Crafts are fun," said Tigger.

"But Tiggers like bouncing

in leaves the best."

"So do Roos!" said Roo.

"No!" shouted Rabbit.

"Please don't make another mess!"

63

"My house is always

full of leaves," said Eeyore.

"It's not so bad."

"So come on, Rabbit," said Tigger.

"Let's get messy!"

Tigger grabbed Rabbit

by the hand and bounced him

into the middle of the pile.

Everyone else jumped in after them.

Rabbit started to giggle.

Then he let out a big laugh.

He liked playing in the leaves!

Rabbit picked up

an armful of leaves

and tossed them into the air.

"Happy fall!" he shouted.

Can you match the words with the pictures?

leaf

Rabbit

rake

pile

Pooh

Fill in the missing letters.

j_mp

c_llage

Pig_et

_ree

groun_

Disney's

A Winnie the Pooh First Reader

Bounce, Tigger, Bounce!

Adapted by Isabel Gaines

ILLUSTRATED BY Francesc Rigol

Bounce, Tigger, Bounce!

Roo was waiting for Tigger.
He was beginning to think
Tigger would *never* come.

Just then, Tigger

bounced up the path.

He bounced so hard a big blob

of snow fell off the roof.

PLOP!

It landed on Roo's head.

"Hi, little buddy," Tigger said.

"Are you ready to go bouncing?"

"I am! I am!" Roo cried.

And off they went.

Tigger took big bounces, like this:

BOING! BOING! BOING!

Roo took little ones, like this:

BOING! BOING! BOING!

Tigger and Roo bounced

deeper into the woods.

Soon they came to a tall tree.

Roo looked way up

into the branches.

"Can Tiggers climb trees?"

he asked.

"Climbing trees is what Tiggers

do best," said Tigger.

"Only they don't just climb them.

They *bounce* them!

Here . . . I'll show you."

Tigger bent down, and Roo
hopped onto his shoulders.
Up the tree they bounced.
BOING! BOING! BOING!

Soon they reached

the very top.

Tigger looked down.

His head began to spin.

83

Suddenly, Tigger's tail

felt funny, too.

Roo was swinging

back and forth on it.

"S-s-stop that," Tigger begged.

"You're rocking the forest."

84

Just then,

Pooh and Piglet came by.

"HELP!" Tigger yelled down.

"Tigger!" Pooh yelled up.

"And Roo!

What are you doing up there?"

"Tigger is stuck," said Roo.

85

Pooh and Piglet hurried off
to get some help.
They came right back
with Kanga, Rabbit, and
Christopher Robin.

"Tigger is stuck," Roo

told his mother.

"That's too bad," she said.

"No, it's good," Rabbit said.

"Tigger can't bounce anyone

up there!"

"Well," said Christopher Robin,

"we have to get them *both* down."

Christopher Robin took off
his coat.

Pooh grabbed a corner.

88

"Here I come!" cried Roo.

"WHEEEE!"

He jumped right into the coat.

Then it was Tigger's turn.

"Jump, Tigger!" said
Christopher Robin.
"Tiggers don't jump,"
said Tigger. "They bounce."

"Then you'll have to climb down,"
said Christopher Robin.
"Tiggers *can't* climb down," said Tigger.
"Their tails get in the way."
And he wrapped his tail tightly
around the tree trunk.

"If I ever get down,"
Tigger gasped,
"I promise never
to bounce again!"
Rabbit's ears snapped
straight up.
"I heard that!" he cried.

Well, it took a while.

But not forever.

Tigger didn't jump down.

And he didn't climb down.

He just unwrapped his tail

and slo-o-owly slid down the tree.

PLOP!

Tigger landed in the soft snow.

He was so happy to be back

down, he felt like bouncing.

"No, no, no!" Rabbit cried.

"You promised. No bouncing!"

"You mean I can't *ever* bounce again?"

"Never," Rabbit said.

"Not even one teensy-weensy

bounce?" Tigger asked.

"Not even one," Rabbit replied.

Tigger's chin dropped.

His tail drooped.

Sadly he turned away.

Tigger's friends stared after him.

They all felt sad, too.

Except for Rabbit.

He was smiling.

Roo looked from Rabbit
to Tigger and back again.
"I like the old bouncy Tigger
best," he said at last.
"Me, too," everyone else said.
Everyone but Rabbit.

"What about you, Rabbit?"

said Kanga.

"Well," said Rabbit. "I . . . ah . . .

I . . . that is, I . . ."

For once, Rabbit didn't know

what to say.

Rabbit thought about all
the times Tigger had bounced him.
Then he thought about how sad
Tigger seemed without his bounce.
"Oh, all right," he finally said.
"I guess I like the old Tigger
better, too."

Before Rabbit could change

his mind, Tigger said,

"Come on, Rabbit.

Let's you and me bounce."

"Me bounce?" Rabbit said.

"Why not?" Tigger said.

"You have the feet for it."

Rabbit looked down

at his big, flat feet.

"I have?" he said.

"You have!" everyone

else agreed.

Rabbit tried a little bounce.

BOING!

Then he tried a bigger one.

BOING!

Soon he was bouncing

just like Tigger.

103

"Come on," Rabbit cried.

"Everybody bounce!"

And so they did.

They all bounced

together through

the Hundred-Acre Wood!

Disney's
A Winnie the Pooh First Reader
Pooh
Gets Stuck

ADAPTED BY Isabel Gaines

ILLUSTRATED BY Nancy Stevenson

Pooh
Gets Stuck

Winnie the Pooh was hungry.

Hungry for honey!

Now, honey rhymes with bunny.

And bunny means rabbit . . .

So Pooh set off to visit
his good friend Rabbit.
Rabbit always had honey
at his house.

"Come in, Pooh," said Rabbit.

"You're just in time for lunch."

That's just what Pooh

was hoping to hear.

He squeezed in through

Rabbit's front door.

Pooh sat down

at the table

and began to eat.

Pooh ate and ate.

And then he ate some more.

At last, Pooh stood up

and patted his tummy.

"I must be going now," he said

in a rather sticky voice.

"Good-bye, Rabbit."

Pooh started out the door . . .

And then he stopped!

Pooh's head was already outside.

But his feet were still inside.

His big, round tummy

was stuck in the middle.

Rabbit gave Pooh a push.

Rabbit gave Pooh a poke.

Nothing seemed to help.

Pooh stayed where he was.

"There is only one thing to do,"

Rabbit said.

And off he went to find

Christopher Robin.

Pooh waited for Rabbit to return.

He waited and waited.

Finally, Rabbit came back

with Christopher Robin.

Christopher Robin

patted Pooh's head.

"Silly old bear," he said.

Christopher Robin took hold
of Pooh's paw.

Rabbit took hold
of Christopher Robin's shirt.

Then they pulled
as hard as they could.

But poor Pooh stayed stuck.

"There's only one thing to do,"

Christopher Robin told Pooh.

"We must wait for you

to get thin again.

Thin enough to slip

through Rabbit's door."

So Pooh and the others waited.

After a while Eeyore came by.

He looked at Pooh and sighed.

"This could take days,"

Eeyore said.

"Or weeks," he went on.

"Or maybe even months."

"Oh, bother," said Pooh.

"Oh, bother," Rabbit agreed.

Pooh soon got tired of waiting.

Pooh was not happy.

He was hungry!

He got hungrier and hungrier
each day.

That night Gopher popped up

outside Rabbit's hole.

He opened up a big lunch box.

"Time for my midnight snack,"

Gopher told Pooh.

"Snack?" Pooh said hungrily.

Inside, Rabbit heard voices.

He jumped out of bed.

Rabbit did not want

Pooh snacking.

He wanted Pooh thin!

He wanted Pooh gone!

Rabbit ran out the back door.

Just in time.

Gopher was about to give Pooh
some honey.

"No, no, no!" Rabbit cried.

"Not one drop!"

Rabbit grabbed the honeypot.

Then he made a sign

and stuck it in the ground.

The sign read:

DO NOT FEED THE BEAR.

Days passed.

Nights passed.

Pooh was still stuck.

Then one day, it happened.

Rabbit leaned against Pooh,

and Pooh moved.

But just a bit.

Rabbit raced off

to get some help.

Rabbit returned with Eeyore,

Kanga, Roo, and

Christopher Robin.

Christopher Robin grabbed

Pooh's paws.

Kanga grabbed Christopher Robin.

Eeyore grabbed Kanga.

Roo grabbed Eeyore.

Rabbit ran inside

and pushed Pooh's legs.

The others pulled his paws.

Push!

Pull!

Push!

Pop!

Pooh flew out of the doorway

and crashed into a hollow tree.

A honey tree!

Eeyore looked up at the tree.

Pooh's legs were waving

in the breeze.

"Stuck again," Eeyore sighed.

"Don't worry,"
Christopher Robin
called up to Pooh.
"We'll get you right out."

But Pooh was in no hurry.

There was honey above him.

Honey below him.

Honey all around him.

"Take your time,

Christopher Robin,"

Pooh called down.

"Take your time!"